P9-DUU-273

A Christmas Carol

ILLUSTRATED BY MARIE DEJOHN

Lexicon Publications, Inc.
95 MADISON AVENUE
NEW YORK, N.Y. 10016

Ebenezer Scrooge was a mean old man who cared only about money. He made Bob Cratchit work in the cold. Bob needed his job, because his son, Tiny Tim, must have crutches to help him walk. Christmas was coming too. But Scrooge didn't care.

Everyone went home to celebrate the holiday, full of good cheer and happiness. They called out Merry Christmas greetings to one and all.

But Scrooge didn't like Christmas! He didn't like the celebrations, the happiness, and the good cheer. "Bah! Humbug!" was his favorite greeting for the season.

When Scrooge arrived at his house, he put on his nightclothes and crawled into bed. Suddenly, he heard a clanging noise. He looked up and saw the ghost of his partner, Marley, in chains. Scrooge was afraid.

"Three ghosts will visit you," Marley said,
"Heed them well."

Sure enough, the Ghosts of Christmas Past, Christmas Present, and Christmas Future visited Scrooge that night.

The ghosts showed him his past life; how he lived in the present; and what his future would be. It made him want to change his ways.

Morning came, and Scrooge remembered all he learned from the three ghosts.

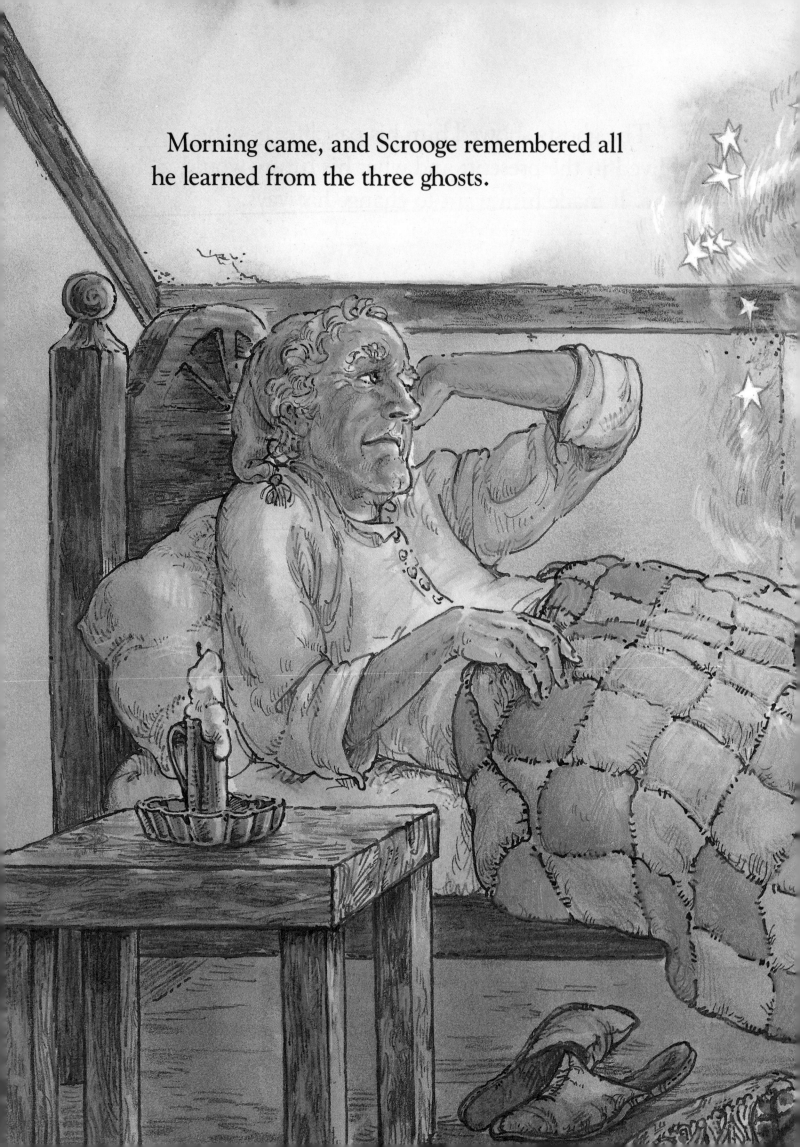

Scrooge got up and danced around with a big smile on his face. He gave a boy money to buy a turkey and take it to the Cratchits' house. Then he put on his coat and went out.

All day long he greeted people with a smile and said "Merry Christmas!" He gave money to the poor and shared with them his new-found spirit of the season.

Scrooge became a kind and generous man who truly knew the meaning of Christmas. He celebrated with the Cratchit family and gave Bob Cratchit a raise.

Tiny Tim spoke for all when he declared, "God bless us, everyone."